Car Wash

Sam Carter

Illustrated by
Dan Chernett

To the youth of Firth Park, Sheffield – JP

First published in 2009
by Franklin Watts

Text © Deborah Smith and John A Pitts 2009
Illustrations © Dan Chernett 2009
Cover design by Peter Scoulding

Franklin Watts
338 Euston Road
London NW1 3BH

Franklin Watts Australia
Level 17/207 Kent Street
Sydney, NSW 2000

A CIP catalogue record for this book
is available from the British Library.

ISBN: 978 0 7496 9038 0

1   3   5   7   9   10   8   6   4   2

Franklin Watts is a division of Hachette Children's Books,
an Hachette company.
www.hachette.co.uk

Harvey, Sam, Amber, Ravi, Jade and Lewis are:

Hi, I'm Harvey!

I live in Carter House with my mum and little sister, Tia.

Greenfield Street

Greenfield Street

Medical Centre

Community Centre

I.

The Crew's bench

Playground

Dalton House

Carter House

Spring Vale Road

SPRING VALE

I love: chilling with the Crew

I hate: wet grass

I want to be: in a famous band

Best word: dinner!

Dove Close

Robin Road

Finch Close

Peck Road

Lark Street

Venn Road

Smith Way

Cole Street

Spring Vale School

1. **Chicken House**
2. **Sleek Lady**
3. **Sun and Sea**
4. **Hot Wok**
5. **Empty shop unit**
6. **8 To Late**

Chapter One

It's the first day of the school holiday.

I'm starved! And skint!

I walk past the Chicken House.

It smells great in there.

"Yo, kid!"

I look round. It's Zed, one of the Cheetas, calling me.

The Cheetas are older than the Crew.

They have cool cars and hot girls.

"Over here!" Zed says.

So I walk over to them.

"Yeah?" I say.

Zed hands me some notes.

"Go get us some food," he says.

"Two buckets of crispy chicken, six chips, six large cokes."

"No problem, bro!" I say.

Cool! I'm down with the Cheetas!

I give Benny the order and hand him the cash.

He frowns. "Cheetas got you running errands?" he asks.

I shrug. It's OK by me.

The Cheetas are the coolest crew around.

No one messes with them!

Benny gives me the chicken, chips
and cokes.

He hands me the change and frowns
again.

"You take care with the Cheetas,"
he says.

I take the food out to their car.

"Here you go," I say.

"Safe, keep the change," Zed says.

"For real?" I ask.

Zed and the other Cheetas laugh.

"Yeah, man – that loose change is nothing to us!" Zed says.

So I take it – and buy my own chicken and chips!

One day, when I'm older, I'm gonna be a Cheeta!

I walk on to hook up with the Crew.

I share my chips and tell them about the Cheetas.

"Man, I wish we had money like that," says Ravi.

"Maybe we can make our own money," says Jade.

We all look at her.

"Yeah, Jade's right," says Sam. "We just need a plan!"

But what?

We go for a walk, to think some more.

Jade points to her dad's car.

"Look at that!" she says, with a laugh.

Some joker has written CLEAN ME on it.

"Mum hates Dad's dirty car," she adds.

Then she stops and looks at us all.

"Are you thinking what I'm thinking?" she asks.

"Yeah, let's sell the car!" shouts Lewis.

"NOOOO Lewis!" we shout back.

He never gets it.

"We're thinking
CAR WASH!"

Chapter Two

We rush back to our bench.

"So what do we need?" I ask.

"Let's make a list," says Jade.

She takes out a little notebook and pen.

"OK, go!" she says.

"Stuff to clean with!" says Lewis. "My mum's a cleaner – she's got loads of stuff."

"Result!" I say.

"We need water to rinse the soap off," says Amber.

"And buckets to carry it," adds Sam.

"We can get water from Hot Wok," Jade says. "I'm sure Dad and Gran won't mind."

"Sorted!" I say. "Let's start tomorrow!"

Next morning, we meet outside
Hot Wok.

"Mum said I could bring this soap stuff,"
Lewis says.

Amber holds up two big yellow sponges.

Me, Sam and Jade hold up buckets.

"And I've made a sign," says Ravi.

"How much shall we charge?" he asks.

We all shrug.

"How about £3?" I say.

"Sounds good to me," says Ravi.

"Same as a Chicken House meal deal."

He writes it on the sign.

"OK, let's go and get some water," says Jade.

She leads me and Sam to the back of Hot Wok.

We fill our buckets from the tap.

Jade grabs a sponge too.

Then we carry them back outside.

Man, the buckets are heavy!

Now we're ready to go.

All we need is a customer!

So we wait.

…and wait!

And WAIT!!!

Chapter Three

"How come no one's stopping?" moans Ravi.

"This is BORING!" says Lewis.

Jade's dad comes out.

"No takers?" he asks with a grin.

"How about you wash my car for free?"

We all stare at him.

This WASN'T in the plan!

"If you do a good job, people will see," he says.

OK. So he has a point.

"How much of that soap do we need, Lewis?" I ask.

Lewis shrugs. "All of it, I think," he says.

He pours the lot into one of the buckets.

I dip a sponge in the soapy water and start washing.

Lewis and Amber do the same.

There are loads of bubbles.

This is going great!

"Er… guys…" Sam calls over.

"I think we have way too much soap!"

I stop washing and stand back to look.

The car is one big blob of bubbles.

We all look at Lewis.

"What?" he says.

He never gets it.

"Better start rinsing!" Jade says.

But it's not that easy.

Two buckets of water rinse away hardly any bubbles.

We take turns to get more water.

We have to fill the buckets again and again.

And again and again.

And AGAIN!

Twelve buckets later, we finish at last!

Jade's dad comes out to look.

"Nice job," he says, smiling.

"But maybe a bit less soap next time?"

Chapter Four

We all flop down on the ground.

"This is BAD!" I say. "We need a rest – and we have no money yet!"

Benny comes over from the Chicken House.

"We're closed!" I say.

"Oh, come on!" he says. "Don't give up. You can use my outside tap – and my hose."

"No more buckets!" I yell.

"Thanks, Benny!" we all say.

Benny laughs his big laugh.

"And if you wash my jeep for free," he adds, "you get free chicken."

We jump back up.

"Deal!"

We move the car wash to outside the Chicken House.

Things are looking up!

And we use MUCH less soap on Benny's jeep.

It's time to rinse.

Sam picks up the hose.

"I'll go and turn on the tap," says Ravi.

Next thing, Sam shouts, "Ooooohh HELP!"

A blast of cold water hits me in the back.

"Arghh!" I yell.

I turn round, soaking wet.

Ravi has turned the tap on too hard.

Sam can hardly hold the hose.

"Turn it off, Ravi!" we all shout.

But Ravi thinks we say, "Turn it up!"

The hose goes mad – spraying all over us.

Finally Ravi turns off the tap.

The water stops.

Ravi comes round the corner.

"Oops…" he says, when he sees us.

Then Amber laughs. "Hey, look at the jeep, guys!" she says.

So we all look. The jeep is gleaming!

"It got rinsed – and so did we!" I say.

Benny comes out with a large chicken bucket.

He gives a big laugh.

"That hose is tricky," he says. "I see you found out the hard way!"

Then he hands me the chicken.

"Great job, guys," he says.

He laughs again and goes back into the shop.

"Lucky it's a hot day!" he calls back.

We all roll our eyes.

Then we tuck in to the chicken!

Chapter Five

Next day, things go much better.

We put the sign up again.

Two minutes later, a car stops to be washed.

We have our first real customer!

Me, Amber and Lewis wash the car.

"We'll put the hose on," say Ravi and Sam.

"OK – but aim it at the car this time!" I joke.

The customer is happy.

She pays Jade £3 and drives off.

Then another car pulls up.

From then on, we hardly stop all day.

And the next day is even better.

The car wash is making a killing!

Jade counts the money.

"£72 so far," she tells us with a big grin.

"We're rich!" Lewis shouts.

Some of the Cheetas watch us work.

I hope they think we are cool.

Two of the Cheetas come over.

Zed and XS.

"You got a good little business here," says Zed.

"Thanks, man!" I say. I'm so happy!

"So, now you pay us half," Zed goes on.

We all gasp.

"Why?" I ask.

"If you don't pay the Cheetas, bad things happen," Zed says.

XS pulls out a crow bar – and swings it.

"Bad things like this!" he says.

The crow bar just misses the car we're washing! The car speeds off.

Zed and XS laugh.

"NOW SHOW US THE MONEY!" Zed hisses.

Jade holds out the money we have made.

Zed takes half and stuffs it in his pocket.

"Keep safe!" he says with a sneer.

Then they leave.

We are all shocked!

We start to pack up the car wash.

"At least we had fun making the money," says Ravi.

"Yeah, I guess," I say.

I sit down on the kerb.

I don't wanna be a Cheeta now. No way!

Benny comes out. "Don't let the Cheetas win, guys," he says. "I'll watch out for you. Trust me."

So the next day we open the car wash.

The Cheetas watch us work.

This time I don't smile at them.

Later, as we pack up, Zed comes over with XS.

"Here they come," Ravi groans. "They're gonna take half our money again!"

Then suddenly, a van pulls up.

Two men get out and start to hook up Zed's car.

They are going to tow it away!

"Hey!" Zed shouts.

He runs back over to his car.

"NO! Please, man!" he begs. "Not my car!"

But the men just carry on.

Benny comes out of the Chicken House.

"Zed never pays his bills!" he says.

The two men wave at Benny.

Then they drive off with Zed's car.

We watch Zed chase his car down the road and we fall about laughing.

Now we can keep all the money from our car wash.

TONY'S TOWS

The Bull

Hot or Not?

"Is that Kai over there?" Jade asks.

I look over.

"Yeah, that's Kai," I say.

My insides feel all fuzzy! Kai is so hot!

"Who is he with?" Lewis asks.

"That's Sasha from Dalton House," says Sam.

"She's well hot!" says Lewis.

Jade pulls a face at me. She knows I like Kai.

"Man that Sasha is hot!" Harvey says.

"Really hot," says Sam.

"Mmm, very pretty," agrees Ravi.

So all the boys think Sasha is hot.

What about me?

Am I hot – or not?

Is Amber hot or not?

Amber loves football. She's the
Crew's star player. She also
likes Kai — and wants him to
ask her out. But Kai
isn't into sporty girls, so Jade
comes up with a plan.

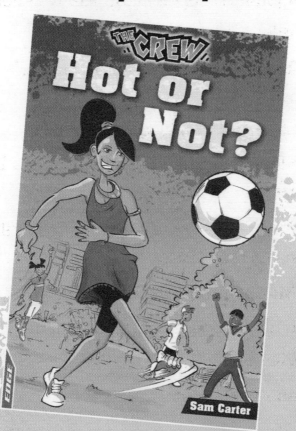

Catch up with all 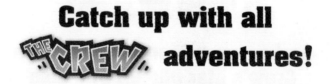 adventures!

978 0 7496 9038 0

978 0 7496 9039 7

978 0 7496 9042 7

978 0 7496 9041 0

978 0 7496 9040 3

978 0 7496 9037 3